For Ella
with love from Niki

BLOOMSBURY
CHILDREN'S
BOOKS

First published in Great Britain in 2001
by Bloomsbury Publishing Plc
38 Soho Square, London, W1D 3HB

A CIP catalogue record of this book
is available from the British Library
ISBN 0 7475 5011 5

Printed in Hong Kong by Wing King Tong.

1 3 5 7 9 10 8 6 4 2

Old Bob's
Brown Bear

Story and Pictures by Niki Daly

BLOOMSBURY
CHILDREN'S
BOOKS

On Old Bob's birthday, Gran gave him a teddy bear.

"But old men don't play with teddy bears," said Emma, watching her grandpa unwrap his present.

"Well, Old Bob always said he wanted a teddy bear," said Gran.

"Why?" asked Emma.

"Because, I never had one when I was a little boy," explained Old Bob.

Old Bob looked at Teddy. Teddy looked at Old Bob. Something was wrong.

"It's very nicely made," said Old Bob.

Old Bob kept saying nice things about his teddy bear. But Emma could tell . . .

Old Bob didn't LOVE his brown bear.

When they had tea and birthday cake, Old Bob squeezed Teddy between his dusty books. Emma got Teddy down and hugged him.

She sat on the floor and fed Teddy some of Old Bob's birthday cake.

When it was time to go, Emma held Teddy very close to her.
Mum said, "You must put Teddy down now, Emma.
It's time to go home."

But Emma held Teddy even closer and cried,
"I WANT TEDDY!"

"You can play with Teddy the next time you visit," said Gran.
Emma gave Teddy back to Old Bob but she wasn't happy.
She saw how Old Bob pushed Teddy back between his dusty
old books.

The next time Emma visited Old Bob, she found Teddy between the same dusty books in the dark study.

"Teddy's been waiting for you, Emma," said Old Bob.

Emma squeezed Teddy. Teddy was starting to smell like Old Bob's dusty books.

Emma and Teddy looked at Old Bob's books.
Emma liked the one filled with photographs. So Old
Bob showed Emma a photograph of a little boy.
    "That's me with the wind up train I got for
my birthday when I was your age," said Old Bob.
    "But you didn't have a teddy," sighed Emma.
    "No," said Old Bob, "and I've always wanted
one of those old fuzzy-wuzzy teddy bears that
are all worn out with lots and lots of love."
    Emma gave Old Bob's new teddy a cuddle.

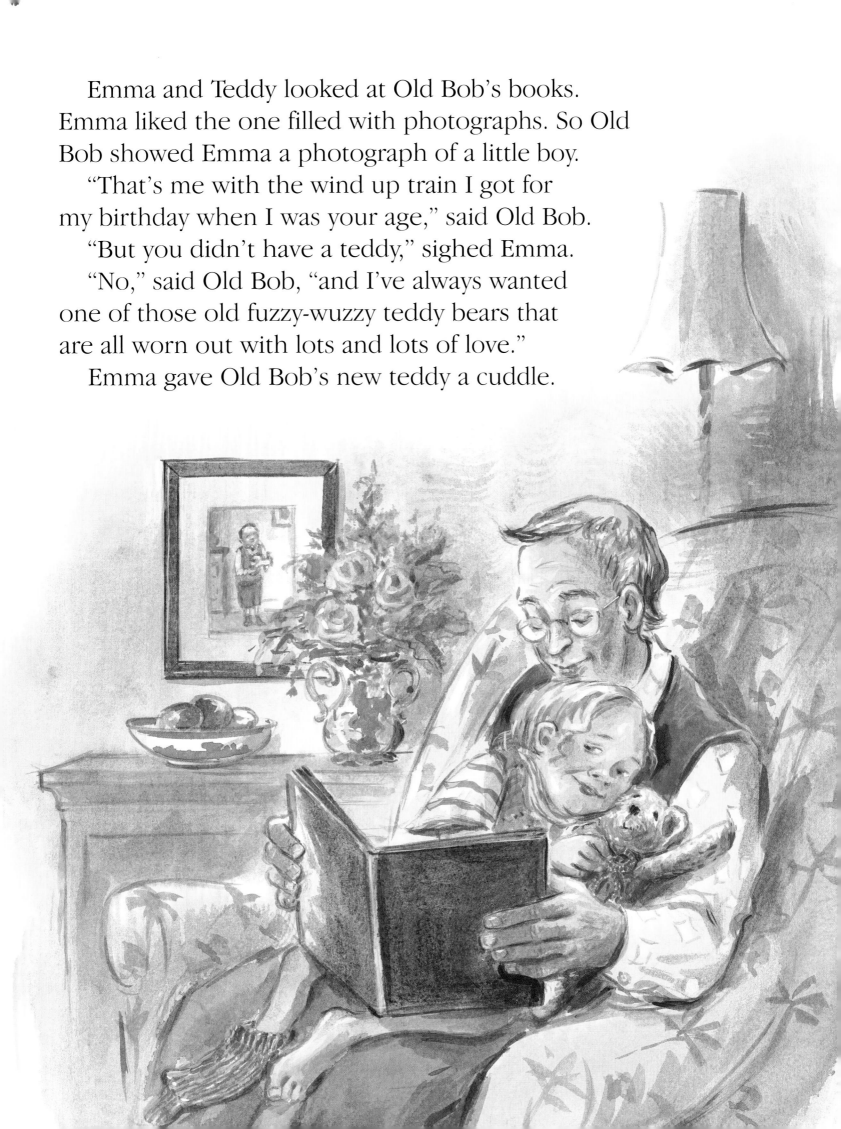

When it was time to go home, Mum said, "Give Teddy back to Old Bob, Emma."

"Teddy will be here next time you visit," said Gran.

But Emma clutched Teddy so tightly that Mum had to tug on Teddy's legs. Still, Emma hung on and wailed.

"I want Teddy!"

"Maybe Teddy can have a holiday with you," said Old
Bob. "And you can bring him back next time you visit us."
Old Bob gave Emma his scarf as a blanket for Teddy.

Teddy had a lovely holiday with Emma. They had
a picnic in the garden with Emma's other toys.
They went shopping.

They went to the beach and got wet and full
of sun cream and sand.

When they got home, Emma gave Teddy a
bubble bath.

After his bath
Emma hung him
up to dry.

When he was dry
she gave his ears
a good brush.

Mum found one of Emma's old baby vests for Teddy.
At bedtime, Emma snuggled up against Teddy.
He didn't smell like Old Bob's books anymore.

When Old Bob saw Teddy again he chuckled, "Teddy must have had a lovely holiday – just look at him!"
Emma told Old Bob all about Teddy's holiday.

But when it was time to go home, Mum said, "Give Teddy back to Old Bob now, Emma. When we visit you can play with him again."
But Emma held on to Teddy and cried,

"I WANT TEDDY!"

"Let's ask Old Bob what he thinks,"
said Gran.
  Old Bob looked at Teddy.
  Emma looked at Old Bob.
It looked as though he was
beginning to love Teddy.
  But Old Bob said,
"Well, perhaps, Emma
can go on looking
after Teddy for me."

When Old Bob waved goodbye he called,
"Come back soon and don't
forget to bring Teddy!"

Emma looked after Teddy for a long, long time. She loved him so much that the fur around his nose and tummy got hugged right off.

When he got all tangled up, Emma brushed the fur on his ears until he looked like a fuzzy-wuzzy teddy bear.

Later, when Emma started school, she didn't see Old Bob quite so often. Old Bob didn't see Teddy for a very long time.

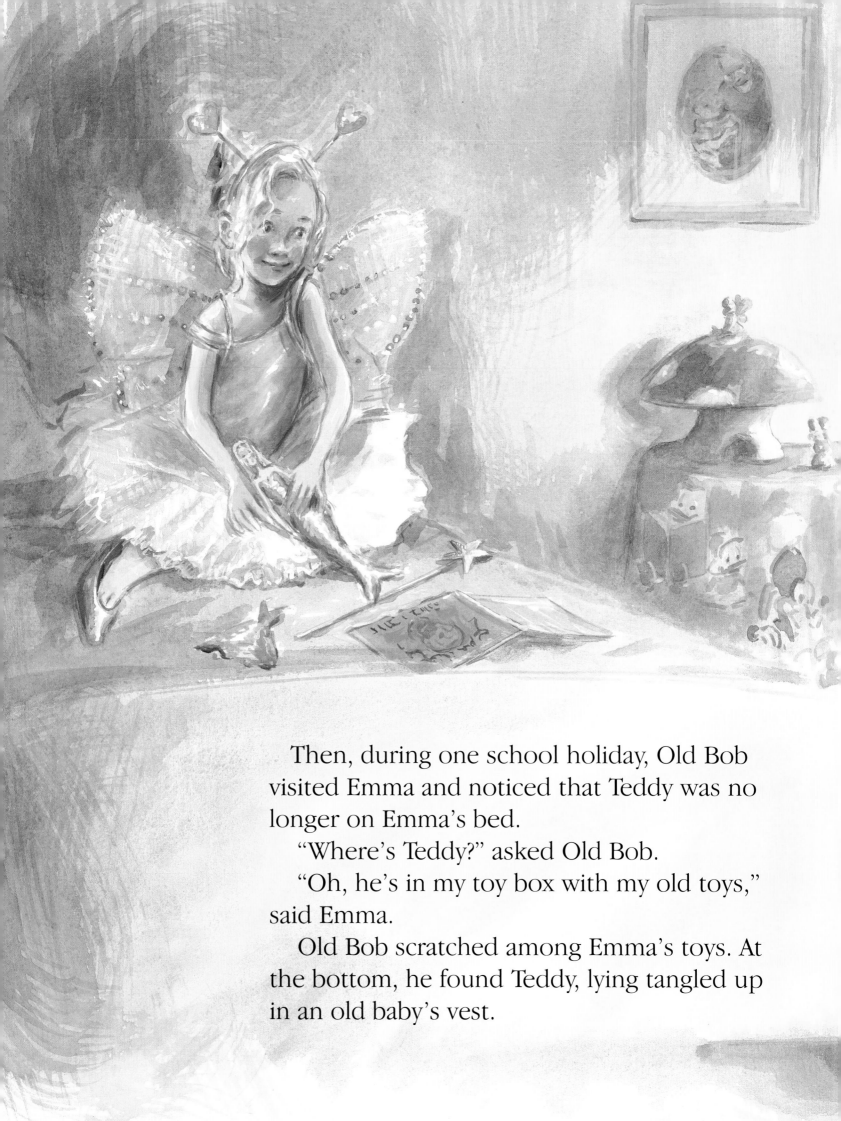

Then, during one school holiday, Old Bob
visited Emma and noticed that Teddy was no
longer on Emma's bed.

"Where's Teddy?" asked Old Bob.

"Oh, he's in my toy box with my old toys,"
said Emma.

Old Bob scratched among Emma's toys. At
the bottom, he found Teddy, lying tangled up
in an old baby's vest.

Old Bob smiled.

"What an old bear you've become," said Old Bob,
patting Teddy's worn out tummy.

Emma stopped brushing her doll's long blonde silky hair and
smiled at Old Bob.

"He's a fuzzy-wuzzy old teddy bear now," said Emma.

Old Bob looked at Teddy.

And Teddy looked at Old Bob.

"I WANT TEDDY!" said Old Bob, suddenly.
When Emma saw the happy look on Old Bob's face, she smiled and said, "That's okay, Old Bob, you can have Teddy. He's a very old bear now."

Old Bob hugged Teddy.
What was that smell?

Old Bob could smell zoo biscuits and sticky fingers. He could smell sweet grass and fruit juice. He could smell salty sea and sun cream. He could smell squeaky toys and bubble bath. He closed his eyes and smiled.

Yes, Old Bob could smell lots
and lots of . . .
love!